CW00871726

1 MONTH OF
FREE
READING

at

www.ForgottenBooks.com

By purchasing this book you are eligible for one month membership to ForgottenBooks.com, giving you unlimited access to our entire collection of over 1,000,000 titles via our web site and mobile apps.

To claim your free month visit:

www.forgottenbooks.com/free126138

ISBN 978-0-483-53805-4
PIBN 10126138

This book is a reproduction of an important historical work. Forgotten Books uses
state-of-the-art technology to digitally reconstruct the work, preserving the original format
whilst repairing imperfections present in the aged copy. In rare cases, an imperfection in
the original, such as a blemish or missing page, may be replicated in our edition. We do,
however, repair the vast majority of imperfections successfully; any imperfections that
remain are intentionally left to preserve the state of such historical works.

THE M.A.C. LITERARY MONTHLY.

Volume 1.
February-May, 1910.

The
M. A. C. Literary Monthly

| VOL. I | FEBRUARY, 1910 | NO. 1 |

To My Love

Anonymous

In the gathering dusk of evening,
  At the close of busy day,
With calmness oe'r me creeping,
  And dull cares all tucked away,
I find my thoughts soon turning,
  As often they've strayed before,
To one whose early learning
  Our days in common bore.
She was ever happy with me
  As we roamed o'er hill and fen,
Plucked arbutus and the daisy,
  Which disclosed our future, then.
Mid the woods and fields we wandered,
  Drifted on the peaceful stream,
Thought that nothing could asunder
  Rend our lives, or come between.
But the darkness quickly deepens
  Into blackness of the night.
As the hours then were sweetened,
  The days now are worn with blight.
Alone, now, my path I travel,
  Driven on by Duty, stern.
Each day a new web to ravel,
  Without one, for aid, to turn.
But, through darkness, brightly shining,
  Symbol of your love, so true,
Gleams a star, our ways defining,
  May it lead again to you!

The M. A. C. Lit

By Bernhard Ostrolenk, '11

WITH this issue, The M. A. C. Literary Monthly, diffidently makes its introductory bow to its readers and contemporaries. Its appearance, modest in mien yet pretentious in bearing, calls forth interrogatory remarks as to its cause and mission. These interrogations must be answered satisfactorily if the Lit hopes to retain a place among the college institutions.

The classical claim, that of "filling a long felt want," can only remotely be urged as the immediate cause or object of the establishment of the Lit. The absence of a Lit was barely realized at M. A. C. Yet, the Lit, though not regarded as a strict necessity, claims to be an indispensable part of the college and well worth the effort it exacts for its publication.

The literary magazine provides facilities to encourage and develop clear and intelligible expression. This is of prime importance to scientific students. The possession of knowledge is of value only when ability to impart it to others, lucidly and concisely, accompanies it. Clear expression leads to logical thinking, which inevitably demands a mastery of the subject.

Furthermore, the literary magazine affords an opportunity for activity to a class of men of a philosophic and artistic temperament. It is highly desirable to encourage such men in their activities, for it is on them that we must depend to set the standards of culture and scholarship, and who will finally aid in the embodiment of our present ideals of science into the literature of the future.

The literary magazine sets a standard of style and expression in the college that is healthy in its influence and an invigorating stimulus for perfection in the use of English.

It also retains for the future the literature produced in college. For many men, who, upon graduation, are immediately thrust into the activities of life, this literature,—produced while still standing with awe and admiration before the gigantic revelations of the laws of nature that are constantly brought before them, produced, while still eager in search for new truths, produced in the enthusiasm of youth, still filled with phantastic hopes and daring dreams,—

this literature does not receive an opportunity for continuation until later in life, when a review of former achievement may stimulate to further activity.

With these introductory remarks the literary magazine feels its presence justified and purpose explained to merit the recognition and support of the college. As soon as attention is drawn to it, it begins to meet a distinct need in supplementing other college activities.

The Encounter

By Royal N. Hallowell, '12.

THE Dean of the college sat quietly erect in his office chair. Opposite him young Hammond went on with his impetuous monologue. To the end he spoke well. Then the Dean mused aloud:

"Ah, a very young man."

Whereat young Hammond sprang to his feet and forgot to suppress the hot, rash words that came to his lips.

"You can expel me if you wish, but you can't find a single good excuse for doing so. You can't offer one excuse to the students they'll not call pure rot. You measure me with your eye on the fact that I flunked two studies and got into a couple of scrapes; but I measure myself by what I've been to old Mainerd as an athlete and a real man."

"Yes," said the Dean slowly and without emphasis, "we can expel you; but pray be seated, Mr. Hammond, in order that we may consider your case."

With a slight motion of his thin, white hand which was unwittingly obeyed the Dean directed Hammond to a seat. His gray eyes kindled and commanded silence.

Then, during a long minute, the Dean gazed at his office walls as in deep debate over the matter at hand; after which he unlocked one of the drawers of his desk and, taking out a small, flat package, laid it at his elbow.

"Late in the seventies," said the Dean, at last, "I was at Stoburn—not a large college, you know, but famous. I was on the crew—at six. We rowed well and won often.

And the victories turned my head so that I forgot that I was in college to do anything more than row. But one day the President called me to him and said that I could go—that the college didn't need me after all."

The Dean paused and patted a stray, white lock of his hair into place, the movement of his arm suggesting big, sturdy muscles still moving evenly beneath the coat that loosely draped his broad shoulders.

"I was a senior—like you—when they turned me away," he said.

"In the going I lost much, most of which I have made up for; but not all."

Here the Dean picked up the little package at his elbow and, after removing its wrappings, held up a daguerreotype— such a picture as was common in the late seventies—the picture of a young woman dressed in a manner peculiar to the time; which, however, lost no interest because of a poke bonnet and a voluminous old-fashioned skirt.

"In the going," said the Dean, "I lost her."

He flushed and paused. But after a moment, his face regaining its accustomed pallor, he went on:

"Of course I could not row in the final race of the season against Haverford. When the two shells came down the course I stood among our boys—with the boys but not one of them. And, though a fallen hero, I thought they still worshiped me; now I know they only pitied."

"We looked up the water-way perhaps half a mile and saw Haverford leading by a length."

"Then the boys turned to me: 'Gad, old man, we needed you at six to win.'"

"But as we watched, I spitefully hoped that Haverford might indeed win to prove that I could not be dispensed with. Stoburn shot into the lead and finished strong and well ahead."

"So much for the race," said the Dean.

"One impression of the day, however, has fastened itself most powerfully in my mind—not a very tangible impression, for I have always tried to realize it as it came to me then. It rises out of the moment when I stood on the boat-house landing and saw our big captain helped from the shell; the captain rowed stroke. As he rose to his feet he tottered and leaned heavily on the arm of the coach, for he was all played out."

" Now, when he was fairly on his feet, there came the great, deafening Stoburn yell, which I have never listened to since—with his name. It was for the fellow at whom, within a week, I had sneered, partly because he was a scholar, partly because he had refused to blacken his fingers with a little of my own deviltry."

"I turned and went jauntily away. But, as I went, listening to the cheers and to the echoes which clamored with them, I admitted—indeed the admission and the memory of it, has made many things clear to me—'Such a man is a better man than I.' "

The Dean leaned back in his chair. In one hand he held the daguerreotype tightly, with the other smoothed the wrinkles which creased his white forehead. He spoke more and more quietly, more gravely—to himself. He had quite forgot the one who tensely listened. Less and less of the late afternoon sunlight came through the office windows and · the office rapidly darkened.

"Such a man as he is a better man than I."

Young Hammond could not take his eyes from the big, white-faced, dark-coated Dean around whom the shadows were gathering. He could not prevent the sudden distortion of vision which is the result of intense watching and listening; the Dean's bulky figure assumed greater proportions; its uncertain outlines grew terrifying, and young Hammond could not speak.

The Dean placed the daguerreotype in its wrappings, tying the package very carefully and smoothing its corners with nice precision and deposited it in his desk.

"Oh!" Young Hammond buried his face in his hands and groaned.

Switching the electric light at his elbow the Dean fixed his keen, gray eyes upon the boy.

"Mr. Hammond," he said, not unkindly, "is there anything more to be said in regard to your case?"

"It is as you say—all as you say," was the answer, brokenly.

"Yes," answered the Dean sadly, "it is all as I say."

"Your experience is mine, sir,—will be mine. The girl," he cried bitterly—'she does not forgive me. In her heart she calls me a fool.'

Young Hammond struggled to his feet.

"I will go."

The Dean stepped quickly to the other's side and laid an arm upon his shoulder.

"Not yet," he said, in a voice that shook. "My loss is your gain. You will not go, my boy. What I want to do is to give you another chance."

The Attack

By Dean F. Baker, '13.

THE moonlight shone in through the broad, open window; the ends of the muslin curtains swayed gently in the soft autumn breeze. It was near the midnight hour and the spacious room was the picture of peace. Without, even the leaves seemed overcome and subdued by the influence of the soft moonlight; they hardly mooved in the gentle breeze. Quiet reigned supreme over all the moonlit world.

In the broad path of the pale light, which swept diagonally across the room, stood a large, comfortable looking four poster bed. Its massive lines seemed to harmonize with the solemn stillness. The figure which occupied this stately nocturnal throne stirred uneasily from time to time. A guilty conscience or some terrible dream tormented the troubled sleeper. From one side of the bed to the other the unconscious form rolled in vain endeavor to flee from the disturbing thoughts. As if flight had proved futile, and the pursued had come to bay, the sleeping figure seemed to grapple with the foe; the fingers spasmodically gripped and released the bed clothes, then wiggled convulsively to and fro.

Suddenly the form sprang upward to a sitting position. The drawn, pale face of a middle-aged man turned nervously this way and that; his wide open and frightened eyes taking in every detail of the large moonlit room.

George Keen did not sleep well these nights; business was poor and on the verge of a crisis. In addition, midnight visitors who disdained to enter by the front door, through which the weak, nerve-broken possessor of sullied millions so often passed, had for several nights made this and the neighboring village their lucrative hunting grounds. The situation would have worn on the nerves of a much stronger man.

Keen's tense figure remained as still and motionless as a graven image. Every nerve was drawn taut and near to the breaking point. The short, gray hair stood almost on end from terror. The overstrained ears had heard a soft sound on the roof of the one-story side extension. This was followed by a similar sound from the roof of the porch which was built in the angle formed by the house and extension. This porch was directly below his window. Another sound from each direction and then there was silence.

The white pseudo-statuary occupying the four poster grew more rigid and still; the eyes and ears strained in the direction of the broad, open window; the hands gripped the clothes in a wild frenzy. Two minutes passed; the silence became awful; the breeze ceased to move the curtains. Not a movement or a sound came to relieve the taut nerves.

But not forever thus. Another soft sound on the porch was followed by a similar sound from the extension roof. The trembling, feverish hands of the man within groped blindly beneath the bed pillow. Then the shining steel of a bulldog revolver flashed in the moonlight. The sight seemed to reassure the owner. The figure became less tense, although the eyes and ears remained alert.

Again the silence became almost shatterable. The moon soon disappeared behind a passing cloud; the room darkened. The alert nerves of the watcher brought him almost to his feet on the bed; the revolver swung quick as a shot toward the window. Before the trigger could be pulled, the light again streamed in; all was peace.

A second later, two faint, almost inaudible steps, not to be detected except by the overstrained ear drums of the nervous watcher, were heard on the porch roof. This was followed by a slow, steady advance of similar steps from the extension roof. The taut nerves and the straining ear drums caught the slightest sounds. A nerved imagination enlarged these to mammoth proportions.

Keen could stand it no longer; he stepped cautiously from his bed and moved slowly toward the window. The steps on the roof advanced as he advanced. Those on the porch ceased; the maker seemed to be listening. Just before reaching the window Keen stopped and waited. Standing close to the wall, he cocked his revolver and leveled it about waist-high across the window. All movements ceased within and without.

A loud, sharp, familiar sound broke and shattered into thousands of microscopic specimens that ominous and carefully constructed silence. This was immediately followed by another similar wild note about half an octave higher. A rush, and then quiet became an unknown quantity. Flats and sharps became one glorious "hash."

One look of relief, then rage, swept across Keen's countenance. Shoes, the old familiar weapons for such old familiar sounds, remained despised beneath the bed. A revolver spat out into the moonlit air. Two swiftly-moving streaks of shadow, never before honored by such a respectable attack, fled tumultuously in two directions. Keen moved angrily back to that comfortable four poster. The moon looked steadily upon the world. Peace reigned again supreme.

Winter

By Walter Roe Clarke, '10

The frozen moan among the elms,
  The distant mountains, bleak and bare,
Song birds gone to gayer realms,
  All tell again that winter's here.
The creak of ice in frozen might
  Awakes the snow flakes to their task.
They steal upon us in the night
  Like ghosts from out the past.
December's beard was long and white,
  Like ancient patriarchs of lore.
He rode, from yesterday's fair night,
  To the mystic land of never more.
The snow has deck'd the lofty pines
  With glistening gems, so white and clear.
All Nature's bells ring out, in chimes,
  Her old, old story, that winter's here.

The Desert

By Albert W. Dodge, '12

ABOVE, a cloudless sky, deep blue and fathomless, flecked with color only at the rising or setting of the burning sun. Beneath, an interminable desert, arid and dust beaten, choked with sage bush, prickly pear or the sand worn cactus, fluted and gray-green. A lifeless region, shunned and feared by man and beast. There the wind blew the sand in whirling clouds and the unbroken silence seemed mutely to whisper of death without future or hope. Beyond the overwhelming stretch rose the foot-hills, piling up and up; their summits seemed to form the roof of the world ; above them towered still higher the mighty mountains, blue-black, huge and forbidding. Their summits glistened with the everlasting snow, and down their seamed and broken sides ran shining ribbons, life-giving water, that never reached the parched and heat-tortured earth below.

This was the desert that confronted the miner of '49; this the desert that lay like a taunt to the restless energy of the American people, daring them to interfere with its endless death and silence. At last there has come a response and the voice of the West, so full of possibilities and development, is sounding again its call of adventure and wealth unlimited. The desert sand, gathering its fertility for ages, needs but the touch of the water to yield its wealth in a manner far beyond the wildest dreams of man. This great task of reclaiming for the benefit of all the race these thousands of square miles has been given to the American people and they are responding nobly, wresting their reward from the lifeless dust that up to now supported only straggling brush and cactus.

It was on December 3, 1901, that President Roosevelt sent his message to Congress recommending aid to irrigation and the national control of water supply. Seven months after, Congress enacted the most beneficent legislation since the Homestead Act of '62' and the Reclamation Act became history. In 1905 water was turned on 50,000 acres of the thirsty land of Nevada. This, the Carson project, marked the beginning of the ceaseless activity that has dug 1,881 miles of canals, some that carry whole rivers like the Truckee in Nevada and the North Platte in Wyoming. Dams like Minidaha in Idaho have been built, until now 281 impound the water on hundreds of rivers and a thousand flumes carry it to millions of acres of land.

Throughout the ages the desert has been calling. Its fruitfulness has been silently gathering, and the ceaseless struggle for life in that "land that God forgot" has changed the scant vegetation until, as C. G. Blanchard of the United States Reclamation Service put it, "everything that grows is covered with a thorn, and everything that crawls is deadly." Now all is changing; the valleys are bright with golden wheat or green with waving corn. The orchards are breaking under their loads, and comfortable houses dot the stretches where the desert had held its sway and lonely coyotes had bayed at the glittering stars. Truly "the desert shall bloom like a rose" and to the American people shall be the credit and reward.

The Old Woman's Shawl

By Josiah C. Folsom, '10

HENRY DANE'S painting and papering shop lay on the outskirts of the town at just the place where town and country merge. Around it were clustered several of the homes of humble suburban dwellers. The old shop was a relic of days when Springdale had been more of a small country town. On stormy days in winter, it was not unusual for a group of old cronies and neighbors to gather around Henry's big shop stove, tilt back in their wooden chairs and arrange their feet on the high rail which circled the outside of the firebox. Pipes were lighted, coats thrown open and thumbs stuck into the arm-holes of vests. With lower man made happy, tongues began to wag as they can only in an old New England cross-roads store among a congenial group of "old timers."

Today the usual stormy-day group was settled around the fire. Bitter cold, drifting snow and howling winds kept most workers inside. So today Henry was busy, or rather his men were busy mixing paints for the next fair day's work, and overhauling equipment, putting a touch here, making a rearrangement there. They were not hurrying. From his chair at the stove Henry was leading the story-telling and they were as interested in the boss's stories as was anyone else.

"Say, Hen," called one of them, his paint paddle resting where it had been for the last five minutes, "what was that story you was telling Jim Dugren the other day about you 'n' Jake Twomey in the war?"

Henry twisted his portly form around in the chair until he could look over his spectacles at the speaker. His big voice boomed forth.

"Don't you mind nothing about Jake Twomey or me just now. You get to mixing the old yaller for Fred Keene's house. You savve?"

The man winked at the others and began slowly stirring the mixture.

"Beats all how blamed crazy that fellow will get to hear stories when he ought to be at work," the boss remarked, as he turned back to the group. He pulled meditatively at his pipe for a little.

"Come on, Hen, you're ready to tell us all about it now." This came from one of the circle at the stove.

Hen removed his pipe.

"Well, I s'pose so, Bill. You fellows all know old Jake Twomey, of course, how nigh played out he is. You wouldn't believe he's two years younger'n me. But he is. An' you wouldn't think that he uster be as much stronger than me as I am than him now. But he was, just the same. It gets me how a big strapping giant like he uster be, could ever get into the wretched shape he's in, and a little ailin' chap like me ever get into the shape I'm in today. Aint a man in the country as can do a better day's work'n me. I'm sixty-one and there's no bragging is there, boys?"

The "boys" murmured a unanimous assent. Henry removed his pipe again, spat straight through the open stove door into the fire and began again.

"I guess I may as well tell you what I was telling Jim Dugren, how I just about owe my bein' here to Jake. It was down in the wilderness campaign in '64. We'd been fighting back an' forth in the bush an' swamps for weeks, an' I was just about played out with it all,—fever, chills, an' fighting, an' what not. One day we'd been lyin' in the trenches an' water until I was near dead. I guess I'd 'a' giv' up if it hadn't been for Jake. He was next to me an' was takin' it all as cool an' pleasant as a clam. Hey, there, if that isn't him now! How are you, Jake! Come in an' draw up your chair! Lots o' room for another."

A bent old man had opened the door a little and slipped through from the outside. He approached the stove almost timidly, feebly shaking the snow from his worn old overcoat and rubbing his ears. He returned the greetings of the circle. Someone drew up a chair for him and he sat down next to Dane, rubbing his knotted hands.

"Well, Jake, how's yourself?" Henry beamed on him. "An' how's the old woman nowadays? Same's ever?"

"Oh, I guess so, Hen. The old woman's as cheery as ever, don't complain nor nothin', but I'm most chilled to the bone."

"You're only half dressed, man. Why the dickens don't you get you some warmer clothes?" Henry asked as he stopped.

"I—oh,—I don't know as I can. I don't seem to get the money to spare, an' I dunno as I oughter 'til——"

"Aint you got the old woman her shawl yet?"

"N—no, not just yet. Purty soon, though."

"That's what you've said the last six months, Jake. You've talked shawl the last year, an' now here 'tis she a-needing it if she ever does, an' you a-needing it a sight worse."

"It's hard, somehow, Hen, to get enough for it, a-tween payin' for coal an' rent an' to live. It takes the money."

"You bet, Jake. Say!" as he reached into his pocket and drew out a coin. "Put that into the old woman's fund for my sake." He offered a half-dollar.

"No, Hen, thanks just the same, but I'm a-goin' to earn this for her." The old man was too proud to accept anything hinting of charity.

"I say, Hen, how about that story of you 'n' Jake? You was goin' to tell us something about you an' him in the war times." Someone in the circle spoke.

"Sure, talk of the devil and up he comes, as we have seen here. Jake, I was tellin' them about how you treated me that day down in the Wilderness. Let me see, we'd been in the trenches all the day an' I was all petered out. And when the relief came up I was too sick to go to the rear. Jake, he says to me, 'Hang on old chap, an' I'll see what I can do for you.' And a bit later he comes up with a tin bowl of stewed beans and peas and some beef broth. They'd been out foraging an' the company got a treat that they didn't get once in months. Jake made me eat it all, an' I tell you it was the bracer that put me on my feet. Nothing ever tasted so good as that stuff. An' I found out afterwards that Jake didn't save any for himself. He gave all his to me. An' you went off an' cried about it, didn't you, Jake, old chap?" And he slapped the old man's knees a resounding slap. The latter nodded with a sort of sheepish smile.

The talk rambled off to other things.

Soon Twomey rose and started slowly for the door as if unwillingly.

"Not goin' out again into this storm, be you, Jake?"

"Yes, I got to. Got to do an errand for Doc Butler."

"Hold on there. How many errands you gettin' now-a-days. Say, by the way, what kind of a shawl you got your eye on for the old woman?"

"That five-dollar one in Kidder's window."

"Maybe you come around to Keene's tomorrow when I'm painting an' I can give you an errand at the shop here."

"Thanks, Hen, I'll see." And the snow swirled in as the door sprang open and slowly closed.

*   *   *   *   *   *   *

The old man went his way, patiently plodding through the cold and snow day by day, picking up his dimes and occasional quarters by doing errands wherever he could find them to do. The little hoard grew discouragingly slowly. Now it looked as if another week would see it the full five dollars. Errands were plenty and paid well. Again it grew smaller. Reverses were met. No one wanted errands done, no snow shoveled, no parcels carried. Or, something had to be bought to support the life of the old couple.

After one particularly discouraging week Jake went around to Henry's shop in hopes that it might be open and he could go in and warm himself. The front door was locked. He was about to turn away when he thought he smelled smoke. A second thought, and he was sure of it. And it was the smoke of burning paint. Then a faint crackle of flames reached his excited ears. The shop was on fire!

"Fire! Fire! he cried feebly, as he ran back around the building to where he thought he could get a timber and break the windows there. But no. Everything was frozen solid after the rain and freeze of the second day before. So he attacked the glass with his bare hands. It broke with a crash. Smoke poured out and he could see a dull red glare under it. He scrambled through the opening, cutting his hands and legs painfully on the jagged fragments in the sash. But he did not notice. He seized a pail, ran to the faucet and turned on the water. He hastened as he had not been able to do for years. The smoke choked him. He could not half see for the tears in his eyes. How slowly that pail filled itself! How the fire seemed to gain in spite of his efforts! Why did not someone hear his cries and come to help? His efforts were beginning to slacken from exhaustion so soon! He was about ready to drop, but he kept feverishly at work. He was crying with pain and grief. Suddenly the fire seemed to rise around him and the building to crash in on him!

*   *   *   *   *   *   *

Jake opened his eyes and tried to spring up. A cry was on his lips.

"You lay still, Jake. It's all right. You saved the shop. Much as ever I saved you, though, you old hearty!" Henry forced him back onto his pillow.

Dr. Butler came to the head of the bed and laid his professional hand on the injured man's forehead.

"You did well, Jake. You're coming on finely. Just take it easy."

Jake began to feel his burns and cuts. His honest old mind began to think of the bill the doctor would have. It was half to himself he murmured brokenly, "And there goes the old woman's shawl money. Another ten cents would have just made it."

"Come on, Jake," spoke Henry, "you quit your worryin' an' cryin.' I've fixed it all up with the doctor and here's the old woman. She wants to show you that new shawl she's got."

The M. A. C. Literary Monthly

The subscription price of this magazine is $1.00 a year. Single
pies, 15 cents.

Contributions are earnestly solicited from all undergraduates.
l contributions should be addressed to the Editor of The M. A. C.
terary Magazine, and should be in his hands before the 12th day
the month.

tered as Second-class Matter, Feb. 1, 1910, at the Post Office,
Amherst, Mass.

Editorials

E are glad to submit to you this first issue of The
M. A. C. Literary Monthly. We are here by your
consent and by your judgment of good things. We
have your financial support, and what we crave now
your indulgence and sympathy while we are yet in an
ıbryonic state. That you will give us what we desire we
not doubt.

The magazine at present is small. We have not the
ıancial support of many pages of "ads." Depending for
e remainder of this year almost entirely upon subscriptions,
: preferred to start small. Better a small beginning, un-
mpered, than a large beginning struggling 'neath the
ight of debt. It will be our earnest endeavor to make
is magazine representative of the literary side of our
llege interests, and a credit to our Alma Mater. We are
ıall now,—but watch us grow!

*   *   *   *   *   *

HAT should be the end of this magazine? What
the acme of our endeavors? To discuss the questions of a more ethical nature which directly concern
you and me, to keep before us the ideals which
vern our actions, to awaken and increase a taste for things

beautiful, to arouse a greater interest in matters literary, and to help in our way to build up a stronger feeling of fellowship among us all.

*   *   *   *   *   *

THE problem comes before us: What sort of material shall constitute our literary magazine? Shall we discuss at length topics which are before the public eye, or shall the magazine be composed largely of fiction? It seems to us that the former should have no place in our Lit except as we can draw valuable lessons from them. Purely plot stories will have their place, for worthy endeavor in this line is very commendable. We all are much interested in the work of our college mates, even though we are aware that there are a number of professionals in the field who can furnish us in the popular magazines more interesting matter. But the material which is going to appeal to us most,—the material which will be of most good to us, will be those articles, essays, or stories which shall deal with the problems of college life, with character, with culture, with ideals, with the appreciation of things beautiful, with the development of manhood, and with training for the active life which is to come.

*   *   *   *   *   *

THE board at present consists of five members. Future members will be chosen by the board. Elections will be made according to the literary ability of the candidate and the interest he has shown in contributing.

*   *   *   *.   *   *

YOU are all urged to send in contributions, which should be signed. Do not be discouraged if your contribution is not printed immediately. If accepted it may possibly be filed for a future date.

In any case your endeavor has been a real help to you, and your next effort may be a ".first rater."

The

M. A. C. Literary Monthly

| VOL. I | MARCH, 1910 | NO. 2 |

Duet on the Lake

By Leon Terry

Girl's soprano is singing and ringing on high:
 "Only heaven to-day, is more happy than I—
  Sweeter, sweeter, my song than the cooing of dove
 And my heart overflows, so happy am I,
  For my dreams have come true, with the coming of love."

And a deep-chested bass rolls, and calls in reply:
 "Only sunshine to-day, gleams more happy than I—
  Stronger, freer, my stroke, than the flight of a swan,
 And my breast overfills, when my love is so nigh,
  And I sing like a lark with the coming of dawn."

With a swing and a ring, lilts the girl her reply:
 "Boat skims like a bird over lake blue as sky,
  And a hot breath of wind plays with ringlets of hair.
 Sobs well in my breast, I'm so happy, I cry,
  And from depths of my heart bursts the song on clear air."

And the voice of the youth thrills and fills the deep sky:
 "The swift chasing clouds—they are free, they are high.
  Burns the hot sun my arms, as I bend the strong oar,
 And the glad southern wind throws spray in my eye,
  Singing sweet songs of youth, strife and love's golden
   shore."

The Old Homestead

By Albert W. Dodge

UP from the meadow, white with the slender Jacob's ladder, floated the rythmic clink, clank of a rifle touching up the shining edge of a scythe. To the boy, lying on his back beneath a straggling apple tree up on the hillside, it came mingled with the hum of the earth pulsating under the July sun. He rolled over on his side and gazed down across the field, brown from recent cutting, past the red house tucked in beside the row of huge spruces, by the weather-beaten barn, to the long stretch of meadow, where two men followed each other in parallel courses, laying the coarse, rank grass to the left in long swaths. As he remembered his father's words of the morning, something like a sob came to his lips, choking him for the moment.

Yes, it was true. The old homestead was to be sold. It was to go like the rest of the old country estates to satisfy the greed of some rich man, who would only gloat over the broad acres, caring nothing for its old traditions and stories. The rambling old house would be changed and strange children would play under the spruces. He had watched the other farms ·change hands, but that this farm should be sold—the home where he was born, as was his father and grandfathers for generations—that the broad acres of corn land and grass land, received ages ago by will from the Indians should go, seemed to render him helpless in sorrow.

He felt very rebellious as he saw the cows winding up from the swamp, following each other in single file to the bars. Soon it would be time for he and Shep to marshal them for the last time down the old cow lane to the barn. At present, Shep was leaping vigorously at a red squirrel over on Sandy Knoll, and the sound of his barking came faintly to his master's ears. The boy knew that the squirrel was hanging head down from the tree trunk, just out of reach, profanely and excitedly scolding away at the dog below. The squirrel and he were old friends, for had'nt they robbed birds' nests together?

Bear Knoll, gay with waving corn, lay between, and the boy's eyes glistened as he remembered the old story of how it got its name. The trap that had captured the bear, as he came to the corn field by night, was still in the attic, and the boy had often held it in his lap, forming strange stories from its dents and stains. One day, it had caught his brother by the hand, and the huge teeth had left its scars in many places.

The slanting rays of the sun crept in under the tree, and he changed his position, until he sat with his back against the gnarled trunk, gazing with half-shut eyes out over the valley which lay between him and the hills that marked off the horizon over in Topsfield. The dark green of towering pines dotted the swamp here and there, marking the tiny islands where the wild grapes grew. To the left, Idlewood Lake was lying, its sparkling blue waters hidden by the hills, which seemed to be gathering closely around it. To the right, past Vineyard Hill, with its nut trees and wild apples, the brush-covered slopes of the Commons rose. Scattered here and there among these hills and valleys so familiar to the lad, were the houses that commanded the great estates lying around them. There he had hunted and picked blueberries, there he had learned to love and study Nature. Tomorrow he was to go to the city to live with his grandmother.

"Children are such a bother when you're moving," his aunt had said.

"When I'm a man, when I'm a man." The thought ran rioting through his head. He lay still, with unseeing eyes, staring at the fleecy clouds, set like huge pearls in the blue skies overhead, thinking of the future that seemed so mysteriously to promise him wealth. He would return sometime, somehow, and force the owner to accept a vast sum for the farm, and then it would never be sold again, never!

A woodchuck crept out of his hole, hardly two hundred feet away, and the boy watched him dreamingly, as he gathered in the grass with his little handlike paws, and commenced his afternoon meal. Over on Sandy Knoll, Shep had ceased his barking, and the squirrel had gone about his business of a trouble maker. The lad knew that the collie was making his nightly rounds of the woodchuck holes, and that soon the one near him would have its peace disturbed. The watching lad was not disappointed. Shep appeared, crawling inch by inch through the short June grass, his tail waving and eyes glistening with excitement. Then came the rush—with the usual result of the woodchuck winning by a foot, and the dog venting his rage and disappointment in a furious attack on the hole.

The boy whistled, and the dog came sheepishly over to nestle his cold, wet nose in the outstretched hand, and hear the words of scolding and advice on the art of catching woodchucks. Then, holding the dog's head between his two hands, he poured out his trouble to those brown eyes that gazed up so understandingly into his.

Down in the meadow, the mowers had crossed over for the last swath, that would bring them back nearly to the barn. The cows lowed now and then, as they stood by the bars calmly chewing their cud. Soon the men would be coming up to do the chores and his mother would carry the two shining milk pails down to them and bring back the foaming pitcher of warm milk for the supper. Huckleberry pie and milk—he knew what that meant.

Whistling to Shep, he got up slowly, and with a heavy heart, started to round up the cows. Stumbling over the brown, hard turf of the pasture, he was silent to the frolicing of the dog, which ran here and there, gathering the cows to follow them, as they wound in single file down the old lane. For the last time, he climbed the ladder to the mow of English hay, throwing down the usual amount for the animals and then the rank meadow hay for the bedding. His chores finished, he watched the men as they milked, bedded the horses, and finished the chores at the barn.

As he went up towards the house, he looked up at Vineyard, above which towered white castles of fleecy clouds, glowing with the red and crimson of the setting sun. Shadows were filling the valley, and as they darkened, the gloom seemed to steal over the lad. In the years that he had spent there, he had learned to love the farm, and as he faced now for the first time a new world, he felt vaguely rebellious against something—he knew not what. The sun sank behind the clouds, which rolled in fantastic shapes, like mountains lined with golden valleys. He stopped for a moment and watched, while the rolling valleys and crags changed to crimson and faded to gold and purple, and in the constant shifting of the scene, there came to him at last his first realization of the changes that were to come into his own life. Turning for a last look at the broad farm that was going out of his life forever, silently he entered the house.

Reminiscences

By Isaburi Nagai.

IT was a day in April, fifteen years ago, and it was as mild as today. The blue sky was so deep and exquisite that even Southern Italy's might be surpassed. The lark sang in the sky, the field shone with joy. Green barley and golden rape extended from valley to valley. How we were blessed in the bosom of Nature, picking the violets and dandelions, listening to the song of frogs by the brook. The shadows moved on the hillside, yet we did not care.

Evening came and then her mother searched us out in the field. When we reached the gate of her house, I remember the curfew from the distant temple tolling the Nirvana of the day, and cherry blossoms scattered like snow in the air.

* * * * * * *

It was a day in July. The air was dead and hot. The blazing summer sun shone upon the old castle tower of the feudal lord whom our fathers and grandfathers had served with sword and armor. The tiles of "tenshu" glittered like silver scales, and lizards were passing swiftly along the heated stone walls whose air bleached rough surfaces were mantled with ivy. But, oh, how lovely was the shade of the pine under which we sat! The breeze from the old moat caressed our faces and tangled her stray locks. We gazed at the lilies upon the mirror-like surface of the water and we dreamed a dream of youth.

* * * * * *

An autumn day is silent and sullen. The wings of night are falling. A rosy glimmer tints the distant hill top—a vestige of a parting day.

So it was, the eve when I left the home far away.

Father, mother, friends, neighbors and she, all greeted me and blessed me at the end of the village where the small country railroad station stood. Why were her eyes not as bright as usual? Nay, dimmed with tears?

* * * * * *

The night is cold. The wind is blowing through the bushes and trees. There are no leaves on the trees. Quails in the distance whistle with a melancholy sound. I absently look at the wall. My head is tired. My heart leaps! Here a college town in New England,—beautiful and quiet,—New York and Chicago, as noisy and busy as can be,—the prairie, the Rockies and the Ocean. Yonder Mt. Fuji and my loved home and,—her smiling face.

Flunked Out

By Isaac Coleman

"TOO LATE," I gasped, as the gates at the ferry station of the B. R. B. & L. R. R. slowly swung together, just as I was about to dash on board the boat. I stood peering through the gates at the boat I had so narrowly missed, as it swung around, and headed for the other side. Soon its shadowy outlines disappeared in the blackness of the night, and I was unable to distinguish its lights from those of the various crafts anchored in the harbor, whose lights danced and gleamed in the inky waters, mingling with the reflections of the stars above. I was in no mood to enjoy the view of Boston harbor at midnight, so made my way to the smoking room.

Entering the room, I singled out a seat near several men, who evidently were taking advantage of the protection which the room offered them from the bitter cold night air. The men had probably never met before, yet they were discussing their adventures and escapades as knights of the road as if they had known each other for years. Their conversation rather interested me, and glad of the opportunity to lessen the monotony of a two hours' wait, I joined the group. During a lull in the conversation, one of the men, who perhaps had noticed my interest, turned towards me and said, "Pretty tough to be down and out, don't you think so!"

"I should say so," I replied, not unwilling to get into conversation with the man. "Still, one doesn't mind knocking about during a vacation. Just think of the stories one could have for his classmates when he returns to college."

To my surprise, he leaned forward, grasped my arm, and said, "Young man, beware of classmates."

The peculiar emphasis which he laid upon the word, together with his bitter and mirthless smile, secured my entire attention at once. He drew me to a seat away from the others, and sat down at my side.

"Once I was in college," he began in a calm voice. "I applied myself to study, and made a good record. I made many acquaintances and a few intimate friends. The mid years I passed with flying colors. About this time, I became intimate with more fellows, who made it a practice to drop into my room almost every evening. At first I did not like it, for they prevented me from studying; but they seemed pretty good chaps and I soon began to look forward to their coming. They used to ridicule what they called my principles. I was particularly opposed to drinking intoxicants, but they used to tell me that I would not be a man until I took a glass or two. I used to laugh at them, confident of my own strength to resist any temptation.

"One Saturday night we were celebrating a football victory, and in some way, I found myself in a barroom with the boys. Before I knew what they were about, they had ordered some whiskey for me too. I endeavored to refuse to drink, offering my whiskey to another, but this called forth such a string of jeers and taunts, that I drank the stuff. After that night, I drank occasionally; but as time went on, I drank more often. I though I could control my appetite, and frequently preached against the fellow who did not know when he had enough."

"Poor fool that I was, I began to neglect my studies and to find enjoyment in those trips which had been so abhorrent to me earlier. I did not make a creditable record the second semester, but I managed to get through."

"The following year saw me back as a soph, and in with the same crowd of fellows. I spent a great deal of time in the hotels and barrooms and earned the nickname of "Sport." I just barely got by the mid years, and that brought me to my senses. I resolved to turn over a new leaf and give up drinking. My friends would not hear of me leaving their circle, and ridiculed my resolutions. After holding out against them for some time, the craving for drink became so strong, that I went back to dissipation and drinking. Studies were forgotten, notices of low standing from the dean's office were ignored. Of course, when the exams came around, I was unprepared and could see nothing but failure ahead of me. I bitterly repented my actions, but of course, it was too late. Again my class-mates came to my help. They let me take some notes on the exams, which they had prepared. I resolved to use them, vowing that if I passed, I would reform. I had never cheated at an exam before, and I was so clumsy in using the notes, that I was caught. I was expelled. My friends deserted me, and my parents died, their death hastened by my disgrace."

'I secured a job in New York, but one of my former friends exposed me to my employer, and I was discharged. I had no recommendations, and was unable to secure any other work. The girl I had hoped to make my wife married another. The final blow was too much for me, and I gave up. I began to drift from one town to another, from bad to worse, until now I am homeless, friendless, penniless."

The muscles of the man's face became tense, and his jaws set, while an expression so full of hate appeared in his bleary eyes, that I involuntarily shrank away from him. The man's voice died down to almost a whisper, as he finished his story. His head sank on his breast, and he seemed lost in the memories of the past.

Suddenly a low whistle sounded in the room. The man sprang up, and in company with the others, dashed for the door, just as an officer came into the room.

"If I catch any of you around here again," the officer shouted after the hurrying men, "I'll lock you up." "Those fellows have been hanging around here for over a week," the officer continued, turning to me. Guess you'd better hustle on board if you want to get on the other side tonight."

The Aztec Mirror

By Raymond J. Fisk

WE were lost!
Ever since crossing the brook I had suspected it. All day we had been toiling through the jungle, sometimes gaining several yards with slight exertion, again winning but a few feet after great labor.

Now the forest had become wilder than ever. The trail was but a trace, and I was often at a loss where the guide appeared so confident.

We were lost. Pedro acknowledged it. I could not blame him, but two questions demanded answer: it was late in the afternoon and we must make preparations for the night, and the impending storm necessitated shelter.

A particularly oburate bit of underbrush, yielding at last to my machete, disclosed a huge stone, grotesquely carved into the semblance of a human form.

"Tezcatlipoca!" exclaimed Pedro, groveling before it; for though a staunch parishioner of the padre he was a superstitious descendant of the Aztecs.

"Do you know where we are?"

"Si, Senor, I think so. Cozumel's palace should be on this mound on our right."

A dilapidated flight of steps led up the mound, evidently artificial. Upon its level summit a group of buildings surrounded an open court. Low, thick walled, with roofs— originally of thatch—long since fallen in, they gave dismal, mute and accurate testimony to Spanish occupancy of the country. Once, they had been the abode of Indian kings; now huge trees flourished in apartments where monarchs had ruled in barbaric splendor.

One building, perhaps twenty feet square and nearly as high, boasted the remains of a stone roof. This we made our habitation and prepared for the night and the coming storm.

Although flat-roofed without, within, the apartment became a truncated pyramid. Its only ornament was a replica of the idol that had exacted homage from Pedro.

A fire improved the place immensely. After a frugal supper of crackers and hot chocolate we gathered a supply of firewood and settled ourselves for the night.

A few shimmering zephyrs, some stronger puffs and then the storm broke. With all its pent up fury it was on us. A staccato of falling limbs marked its violence. Once, a resounding crash, heard above the general uproar, told of the fall of some forest giant before the onslaught of the elements. Torrents of rain fell as only tropical rain can. Violence, however, proved its undoing, and soon, losing its fury, nothing was heard but the steady drip, drip from the trees.

"Cozumel died on a night like this, the day the Spaniards landed," remarked Pedro, half aloud, half to himself. "Tezcatlipoca appeared to him that night and foretold the ruin of this palace and the downfall of his people."

The fire, throwing into strange relief the fantastic features of Tezcatlipoca, the idol on the western wall, I was struck by a fixity of his expression as though he were watching something before him. Compelled by the force of his gaze to follow it. I noted with surprise that it seemed to rest upon a metal plate let into the opposite wall. As it had escaped me in our hurried survey of the place before supper I investigated it.

It was metal, certainly, possibly bronze, but differing from any metal with which I was familiar by a strange, mottled, misty or cloud-like something that ran through it, defying identification. Over it were scattered blood-like particles, or perhaps they were rust spots.

How populous this deserted ruin must have been, I thought. How often had the shout of the banqueting nobles echoed through these silent corridors.

But tonight silence reigned, broken only by the falling drops without. Could this mute idol but speak how much he could tell me.

Musing thus, linking together fact and fancy, I was startled by observing a movement in the metal plate. It seemed to be reflecting scenes enacted in remote portions of the ruin. The cloud-like mists were in motion, dark, indistinct bodies appeared beneath them, over which swarmed the bloody particles. The picture was vague and indistinct, but becoming clearer and more definite in outline, its significance dawned upon me. Not in a remote part of the ruin was the scene enacted, but in a remote epoch of time.

The twentieth century was forgotten, the fifteenth was supreme. Tezcatlipoca was gazing upon history in the making—history of a people long since forgotten. Pedro's heavy breathing told of his unconsciousness. I alone, a profane intruder, witnessed this revelation to the pagan diety.

The cloud-like objects were sails, the dark, indistinct bodies were vessels, and the mist spots, men. Three vessels were anchored off the shore. Boats filled with men left the vessels, and landed upon the beach. The royal banner of Spain appeared, and a kneeling throng of mail-clad figures proclaim the sovereignty of Ferdinand and Isabella in the heathen land. The white man had come. The Spaniard had landed.

The scene dissolved. The mists and clouds again were busy, the blood-like particles scampered hither and yon. The noon-day sun shone on the pagan city. Stone buildings were everywhere seen. Here and there, pyramidal structures towered above the rest and terminated in a thin stream of smoke, which marked the temples to the heathen gods. Before the palace, a multitude had gathered. A trumpet hushed the noisy babblings of the people. Richly caparisoned steeds, dented but shining armour glistened in the sun. The procession halted and their leader rode forth alone. A solitary figure, clothed with eastern magnificence, advanced toward the lone horseman. Cortes and Montezuma had met.

Tezcatlipoca's muscles quivered, a pale light was in his eyes.

It is night. A storm is raging. Above, the lightning flashes told of battling gods. Torrents of rain hurtle themselves upon the earth. Beneath, men are joined in mortal combat. The Spaniards are retreating along a causeway, pursued by the Indians. On each side, stretches the dark waters of the lake, dotted by canoes filled with the enemy. A cannon's roar marks the annihilation of scores of the Indians, but others press forward. A mounted knight with sword and battle axe is engaged with countless natives with their short sword and deadly maquahuilt, the club with the glass-like teeth. A fortunate blow, and a horse goes down, hurling his rider to the earth. Encumbered by his armour, he receives no mercy at the hands of the light armed native. Perhaps death in the lake ends it, or he is saved for sacrifice. A few broken detachments escape, but it is Montezuma's might against a handful of Europeans. The natives have conquered. The "Noche Triste" has passed into history.

In rapid succession, now the pictures appear upon the magic plate.

The Spaniards are back, Montezuma is a prisoner, the pagan temples smoke with the flames of their own destruction, the heathen gods are despoiled of their golden ornaments and their vestments of precious stones repose in the coffers of the invaders. Montezuma, entreating his subjects to yield, is slain by an arrow. The Aztecs' power is broken.

*　　*　　*　　*　　*　　*

A conquistador rides abroad, inspecting his estate. A group of natives are laboring in the fields—shackles impede their movements. One, lagging behind the rest, attracts the Spaniard's attention. Raising his lash, he brings it down across his shoulders.

A groan bursts from the idol.

Naught but the steady dropping from the trees breaks the silence.

The Senior Meditates

By Royal N. Hallowell

WHAT'S the best thing in the world!" By way of answer, the fluffy cushions in the corner seat swam up to meet highbrow's head, and dimpled in green and white and purple and gold about him, as he lay.

"I ought to be up. You, Jack, switch out that light; it shines in my eyes. Yes, I tell you, I ought to be up; but switch away the light. I worked today—worked."

"Stay awhile, Jack. Softly! Close the door with a bang, confound you! He's gone."

"—The best thing in the world? Let me pull that red canoe girl pillow under my head; Nell sent it from Auburndale—Nell, my love, is like a red, red rose—that's not nonsense—no, neither rot nor nonsense; that's red wine."

"Tonight, old fellow, you may dream a very little, but after tonight, not again. For it has come at the end of four years. Only a few days more to the end. One fact remembered, and a thousand forgot, but be proud of your treacherous, uncertain old head, since it has learned, at least, to think. Only a few days—and then the beginning—no sham this time and pretence of battle—Life itself—God help you on to meet it."

"You, old fellow, have been many kinds of a fool, and you are a few kinds, even now. Four years back—three years back—you were, indeed, a fool. You were a child and, from a man's standpoint, a child is a fool. Your mind was like putty—plastic, it was moulded entirely and always by the flinty, mature influences about it. Do you recall when first you began to cease being a fool and began to be a man? That was two years ago; you listened to the words of a man of mighty influence and profound philosophy, who sought to establish the truth of his thought. And you—little, timid, unadvised boy—in your own mind and soul silently disagreed; for all the processes of your reasoning, all the processes of your imagination and intuition urged you to disagree and to oppose to his, your own constructive idea, although in the light of his mature experience, your presumption seemed as blasphemy before the bar of Truth.

But, in the end, the judgment of your elder was wrong, and yours proved right. Then you saw that you, too, might construct and create; you saw what was the man's part and there began to play it. That was the great mental crisis of your life. "

"And directly upon the first, came a second great crisis. You had always been a good child fool or a wicked child fool, according to your promptings of fear or fancy. But, one day you said: 'I am now my own keeper; I will, here-after, be willing to judge my well doings and ill doings by the standards which God has ordered and which men have proclaimed!' That was again the man's part. And, there-after, as you looked about upon the world, into the blue sky, whose depths and mysteries you could not fathom; then upon the earth at your feet, at the grass and the flowers in their embodiment of the mystery of life, you began to come to a full realization of the man's part and said: 'I would not wish to be a child fool again.' "

"There, smile again, you upper part of my anatomy called my face! If I rubbed you with the palms of my hands and made you flat and smooth, you would wrinkle and smile again, and again. Smile with the joy of your secret— the best thing in the world. But your secret is mine, I gave it to you and you are the evidence of it. Now, let me say once more, just for the joy of saying it and knowing it: 'Old fellow, you have discovered the best thing in all the world—anew and in its entirety! Once, you saw it in the light of your mother's eyes and felt it in the clasp of your father's hand. But today, the fullness if it you see in one other's eyes, whose name you speak reverently and tenderly and passionately. Old fellow, you're not worthy to touch her hand; yet she gives you all.' "

"No, you don't want to lie here and dream. Realities are more glorious than dreams. Today you can begin a life race and win! Life's mountains you can brush away; its forests and waste places you can cross; its deep streams you can ford; its militant hosts you can conquer—for her!"

"Old fellow, your head is hot. Rest for a moment, only, till the fever is out of your blood. Then arrange these pillows prettily; how well their colors blend. Leave them there for some tired head—for some child fool to rest on. Ah, the wonder and joy of the man's part!"

All true happiness, as all that is truly beautiful, can only result from order.

The M. A. C. Literary Monthly

The subscription price of this magazine is $1.00 a year. Single copies, 15 cents.

Contributions are earnestly solicited from all undergraduates. All contributions should be addressed to the Editor of The M. A. C. Literary Magazine, and should be in his hands before the 12th day of the month.

Entered as Second-class Matter, Feb. 1, 1910, at the Post Office, Amherst, Mass.

Editorials

THE welcome given to the first issue of the Lit repaid the Board for its efforts in organizing and producing it. We feel assured that the new institution will prove a valuable asset to our college activities, and, if properly handled, will attain a prominent place in this college.

The Board alone cannot make it a success, however. We need the co-operation of every man who has any ability to write. This is your magazine, and you should need no invitation to make the most of it.

*   *   *   *   *   *

The large attendance at the senior play shows the interest which the students and faculty and townspeople have for dramatic endeavors. The only plays put on in the past few years by this college have been staged through the efforts of the class of 1910. What they have done can be done again, but it seems to us that the stimulus to pay off certain class debts should not be the motive for putting on plays. There should be a college dramatic association which can work up plays of high character and put them on for the sake of their educational value. Such an organization can draw from the entire student body for its talent, and with a live management behind it can book the plays in a number of cities.

Dramatics offer a very delightful field for many who do not take part in athletics or other strenuous forms of college activity, and it offers as much opportunity for training of the mind as does any other part of college life. As a means for getting in touch with people and for making the college better known, it is unsurpassed.

A short time ago a dramatic association was formed, but it is not probable that any attempt will be made to put on a play this season. A course in dramatics under the capable instruction of Mr. McKay will be instituted next year, and without doubt will be a very valuable addition to our curriculum. We hope that active steps will be taken early next fall to develop the dramatic association and make of it a strong feature of our college life.

 *   *   *   *   *   *

What wonder that we love our college. What wonder that our college puts out so many strong men and good citizens. I often wonder if other colleges have as many advantages and opportunities as we do. Granting that they do, I wonder how any man can spend four years within the halls of this college and go out into the word and be satisfied to take a passive part in life's work. For four years we have the glorious opportunity to meet men of affairs, men in all walks of life who are *doing* things, men who are respected and looked up to as the highest types of American citizenship. Always they have carried to us a note of inspiration and have shown us that worldly goods do not bring happiness, that happiness lies only in service to mankind. The more we put into life the more we get out of it, is an old saying, yet its truth has been impressed upon us so that we cannot fail to see its application in our lives and the service which we are to render in the world. What a stimulus these men are to youth just about to enter into life's battle. They make all barriers penetrable, all heights attainable. My thoughts run too swift for my pen—I must achieve results in this world or bow my head in shame before these, my my teachers.

The

M. A. C. Literary Monthly

| VOL. I | APRIL, '1910 | NO. 3 |

The Singing Plow

By R. W. N.

THE time came when John Alfred was forced to give up his studies and leave college—forever.

It was December when he went, and the winds were sweeping bitterly through the valley from the north, mercilessly whipping man and beast with lashes of icy pellets—a fit day, he told himself in rebellious anger, for the ending of a summer's dream; and he laughed grimly as he paced in the cold from end to end of the long station platform or stood looking across the snowy bridge beyond which he had left his life. All the afternoon and all night, the grey swirl of the storm beat against the frost-covered windows of the car, the wind yelled and howled behind the fleeing train; and in the pallid dawn of another bitter day, he clomb stiffly down at his destination.

Hours followed before his father, in the unpainted, ramshackly old farm wagon, came to take him home—it had not been his home for years on years—and he paced them away in the face of the storm's fury, and laughed as even youth can laugh when hell and heaven have come to seem all one.

It was not a joyful meeting. His father pottered at the stringy harness as the young man strode down toward the wagon, and when the greeting could no longer be postponed, came forth reluctant and shamefaced, refusing to meet his son's hard look as their hands came together and parted almost without grasping.

They rode the four miles almost without speaking, and the young man helped to stable the horses before he went in to see his mother—no need to hurry now; she'd see enough

of him from now on, God knew! The dinner was unsavory
and tasteless, notwithstanding the more careful preparation
of it for his coming, yet he ate voraciously and raged in-
wardly to find himself already taking animal delight in so
coarse a feed.   There was no conversation; when reference
was made to his college life, he cried out sharply, "None of
that! It's dead and buried! Never speak of it again!"
and rose quickly and left the room.

When he returned, he had put on working clothes; and
he went quickly out of doors.   He took direction of everything upon himself at once, and went out again after the rude
supper to work at the thousand and one things he found
awaiting someone with foresight to perceive the need of
them and energy to do them.

When he came in at last and sat by the kitchen fire,
he was silent.   The old folks went to bed and left him there,
and he sat until long after midnight, thinking, mourning,
planning.   His college life and his future were dead and
buried; but no man forgets what he has loved, though it
be dead and buried.   And there had been a girl, too—he
had come away without so much as seeing her; what might
have been could not be, and it was better to cut every bond
at a blow.

The bonds were all cut—all but those of remembrance.

He had foreseen the outcome.   Years earlier the farm
had ceased to pay money, and begun to demand it.   When
he had urged new ways and better methods, his father,
querulous and stubborn, had burst into childish anger against
"book-farming;" and this was the result.   When the letter
came from home, telling that foreclosure was to begin, he
had gone into the city to appeal to the manager of the mortgage company.

"Your father's place, and your grandfather's, eh,"
that officer hemmed, "Farmed in your grandfather's fashion,
too."   Then he looked the young man over and added:
"If you want to save it so, why don't you go down and take
charge yourself.   We will hold off a year.   If you get it
started right, we will renew the mortgage.   And that's all
we will do."

There was no choice—and here he was, grimly silent, he
and his work, and there behind was what might have been—
his true work—and the girl.. . . . .

The clock struck one, struck two, and he arose to seek
the little attic pen that henceforth should be his room.   As
he roused himself, he cursed himself and life—quietly, smil-
ingly; and as he passed the cracked, scarred looking-glass and

raised the dusty, oil-streaked lamp to light his face, the reflection showed the calmness of feature that tells of settled grief and settled, inexpressible despair.

The morrow was as the yesterday had been, and the days that followed it showed change in nothing. He ordered the farm work and farm economy, toiling early, late and always, saving, retrenching, spending—and late at night sitting over the puny fire to mourn and plan. To his parents he said little more than what he had to say about the work; when neighbors, especially old acquaintances, came to the place to loaf and gossip, he shunned them when he could, spoke sharply what he must with them, and made them see that to him their room was better than their company. So he was alone at home and was left alone by others at his home. As time passed, he found his hours over the midnight fire becoming shorter, and his grief and despair became more fierce and settled as he saw the sense of them decreasing.

At last spring approached. The wheat fields thawed at midday. Then the brant and geese began to come and (after a few days of picking in them and the fodder lots) pass on toward the north. The redbirds in the peach grove became restless; the number of shrill bluejays in the orchard grew; the crows cawed and quarreled incessantly. Gradually, the thawing of the fields increased and the freezing decreased; grass on southern slopes greened; the willows along the slough lost the brightness of their yellow for a palish green that itself brightened from day to day. The smaller waterfowl went north, at first few and lingeringly, then in many flocks and quickly; and after them, the cranes. He looked at these latter, moving slowly in great V's between him and the sun, and remembered how, a boy, he had listened to their crying and watched for hours the silver light thrown off high in the heavens by their slowly flapping wings. The willows and the maples blossomed, and here and there a violet ventured forth. But day by day, as he saw about him all the changes in which he has been wont to find delight, his bitterness but grew.

The early spring was wet, and April warmth was hastening life when he got into the fields to plow. The breaking had been done the fall before, and he started cultivator plows to stir the ground; his father in one field, he in another. The peach and the plum trees had begun to bloom.

The gentle warmth became a gentle heat, and flinging by the ragged overcoat he had worn, John Alfred rode back and forth across the field, drawing with each furrow nearer the top of the long slope. He came upon it at last and, looking across the land thus brought under view, uttered a sudden exclamation.

The slough along the border of his fields was green and soft with willow foliage up to the very foot of the slopes beyond; and on these slopes great orchards of peach and of plum trees were creamy pink and pure white, and delicate tints of infinite variation between these two, against a dark background of shade-tree foliage scarce unfolded. His team stopped, and he let it stand until he satisfied his gaze upon the blossomed mounds. The sun shone hot. A hawk wheeled all above him. But his momentary forgetfulness passed and he started his horses quickly—and immediately, the plow began to sing.

The sound came from the metal work from which the beams were swung; was not from the griding of the irons, but in the irons themselves. It was monotonous, but not unpleasant. At times it was broken, at times long sustained; sometimes it ceased for but a moment; sometimes for all the length of the field; now it sank into a low vibration, now swelled into a clear tone that swept across the farm; and there was in it the seeming of a content subdued yet permanent. Later, when he thought of this, he thought he must have imagined so; but others heard the singing and found the same seeming in it.

Through all the afternoon the plow sang; and Alfred listened, and looked across to the blossomed slopes, and breathed the odors from them. That night, as he passed the cracked old looking-glass and glanced into it, he stopped suddenly to scan his features. Something was missing-from that he had seen there every night before for months. And in his room he sank back upon his pillow sighing and fell into quiet sleep.

In the morning the plow was silent, but when the day had warmed, it sang again till night. By the third morning, he had come to look forward to the beginning of its song. So days passed. On those when he did not use the plow or it did not sing, he was more restless, sharp, impatient; but in place of the silent bitterness was quick anger and acrimonious retort.

The blossoms on the slopes withered and the trees showed as acres of light green. The plovers had come and were gone, and the great flocks of blackbirds were broken up into nesting pairs. The corn came up, and then began the unbroken weeks of cultivating it.

And the plow sang. Earlier and earlier in the morning

it began, as the days became hotter; more and more it sustained a steady note; and riding on it from morning until night, John Alfred found that more and more his thoughts went out from himself as he listened and busied themselves with the world that was without him.

The blue prairie lilies, the wild-onion flowers, the johnny-jump-ups; the grass, and wheat, and corn; the rabbits hopping by under the hedges; the squalling catbirds, in the branches; the yellow, flitting flax-birds; the thrushes, the crows, the hawks; the cattle in the pastures; the drifting clouds, the playing of sun and shadow,—as the plow sang, he began to notice them, to watch them, to love them for themselves. His father was surprised one day to hear a burst of song from him. The night of that same day, when all the chores were done, the young man sat down with a book, the first time since his homecoming; and he fell asleep with a mis-remembered stanza droning in his consciousness:

> He liveth best who loveth best
> All things both great and small;
> For the good God who loveth us,
> He made and loveth all.

Day after day the plow sang, and day after day its singing drew him more and more away from himself toward the universe. New thoughts, new feelings, began in him, at first vague, indefinite, formless, but developing rapidly toward definiteness and form, and at last his mind filled with the thought and feeling that human progress is as slow as time, and man's part therein but to fill the place he occupies, meanwhile eating, drinking, being merry if he can.

June came—the June in which he was to have been graduated; the June, and the June day. The peach trees on the slopes were already bending with weight of fruit, and he looked across to them, and watched the willow twigs, breeze-shaken, and the stooping, merry pickers among the strawberries. Though he was silent, the plow sang long and clear.

Two days later, his father, coming home with mail, tossed him a roll of papers. Some one had sent him the account of commencement week. He thrust the package unopened into his pocket; and when, alone at night, he tore the wrapper, he lit the papers at the lamp, unread.

A Country Comedy

By Josiah C. Folsom

ONE spring the Haseys sold their big house to strangers and left without so much as telling the names of buyers. So Mrs. Ballard, who lived next door, was all curiosity when a few days later carpenters appeared and spent a week in making alterations. The men somehow neglected to tell her the nature of their work and she considered it rather strange. The next day the strangers were in and getting settled. Mrs. Ballard went about her work with one eye almost constantly on their windows, hoping to get glimpses to satisfy her interest. But one of the first things accomplished was the hanging of curtains, and these were at once arranged to prevent anyone's looking in. The newcomers did not even come over to borrow a tack-hammer or a cup of coffee, something unusual in people at moving time. Mrs. Ballard found herself becoming curious concerning her new neighbors.

The next day the grocer called. He came to Ballard's from the Hasey place.

"Who are the folks at Hasey's?" Mrs. Ballard asked.

"Troop, Miller Troop," Jones told her.

"What kind of people are they? What does Mrs. Troop look like?" she continued.

"I didn't see no one but a big, black-bearded chap, though I heard some women around. He done all the business right at the door. Couldn't get a word out'n him 'bout what they came here for, nothin' but business."

This unprofitable search for information did not satisfy. So when Mrs. Ballard's best friend, Emma Vance, called, the ladies discussed the situation and resolved it became them to call upon their new neighbors. Accordingly they set out.

At the Hasey place their knock was answered by the big, black-bearded man. He did not offer them admittance. Instead, his expression was anything but a pleasure.

"Is Mrs. Troop in?" Mrs. Ballard asked.

"I know no Mrs. Troop. I guess you are at the wrong house," was the unexpected reply.

"But we were told the name was Troop. We mean the lady of the house. We are neighbors here and we thought we would call on her."

"I'm the lady of the house, madam, and my time is fully occupied without receiving callers."

The women were too amazed at this unexpected turn of affairs to say "Good day" before the door closed. Then Mrs. Vance gasped, "What do you think of that?"

Back at Ballard's they discussed the repulse at much length, and at supper time the master of the house listened to his wife's excited monologue.

Then he remarked, "Served you right for your infernal curiosity and gossiping. If they want to be let alone, better do it, Martha." But Martha was not so easily quieted.

For a few days things ran smoothly. One morning the new neighbors started their piano. Someone played awhile, then raised voices were heard and the music broke off. There was nothing remarkable in this except that the big, black-bearded man's voice rose above the others as he apparently interfered. At the first sound Mrs. Ballard ran to her dining-room window where she could hear best through the open windows,

"Well, if that ain't mean in him not to let 'em play!" she commented.

The uproars among the strangers were of almost daily occurrence. There could be heard the voices at the piano which soon became raised in disagreement and the man's voice broke in as he and one of the women quarreled. Mrs. Ballard could understand that the two threatened each other.

One noon, after a morning's disturbance, John heard a detailed and excited report of the untoward doings at the Hasey place.

"I wish someone would interfere," his wife went on, "I don't like such carryings-on. And if that big, black brute hadn't ought to be in jail, then I don't know. Good lands, but such things ought to be put a stop to!"

"For heaven's sake, Martha," exclaimed her husband, "your blamed meddlesomeness and inquisitiveness ought to get hung. Those folks are big enough and old enough to look out for themselves, or else they wouldn't be there. You quit butting in or you'll make a fool of yourself some-day."

The next forenoon Emma Vance came in to gossip. They were discussing the carryings-on at the Hasey place when the piano was heard.

"There now, they're at it again. Come in beside the dining-room window and we'll hear better," Martha led the way.

Voices soon rose and the music broke off. Then above these the commanding tones were heard. When the others had ceased talking, a woman quarreled shrilly and excitedly with him. Suddenly others interfered apparently, for confusion and excitement and uproar rose high. The two women at the Ballard windows sat with strained ears and fearful faces.

"Is it like that every day?" Mrs. Vance whispered.

"Yes," was the reply, "only that's worse than they ever scrapped before. But just hear that!"

For all at once the piano began playing and the quarelling voices changed to a beautiful tenor and a strong, sweet contralto as they sang a rollicking duet. Others joined the chorus.

The bewildered eavesdroppers stared at each other. "Well, if that ain't the craziest yet," gasped Mrs. Ballard.

Thus affairs ran a couple of weeks. Moreover the strangers made no move to meet neighborly acts half way. Rarely did they show themselves outside their own house. Any curtains accidentally open were soon drawn or moved to prevent outsiders from looking in. The loud playing, singing and quarreling went on with little variation.

Why people should be so exclusive and close, Mrs. Ballard could not conceive. And what kind of folks these strangers considered themselves with their unseemly and mystifying noises she could not imagine. Nor did anything tend to clear up her perplexities. John was unmoved by events: he was disposed to let things run their own course so long as he was unaffected. Mrs. Vance was as completely bewildered as Martha. And the Troop people simply added to the mystery.

One morning Mrs. Vance came in again. The women were revolving the neighborhood mystery when sounds from the Hasey place brought them quickly to their places at the dining-room window. The piano and a violin were playing something new. Singers gathered and the chorus swelled. The tenor and contralto led. This stopped suddenly. An excited and unintelligible dialogue between two women broke out. What the trouble was, the listeners could not tell. The excitement gave way to boisterous laughter and merriment. Others were evidently listening and ridiculing. Then the big man's voice came as he wrathfully interfered. For a little, excitement ran high. Gradually participants dropped out until only the man and the woman of the contralto argued. They were plainly at swords' points. Then began the commotion of people running about and others joined in the uproar.

"For the land's sake, what's coming next?" Mrs. Vance whispered.

Her question received an unexpected answer. The man's voice rose above the others as he shouted, "Stop, woman! or I'll——" The rest was drowned in screams. Suddenly two shots rang out and all was silent.

For a moment the listeners in the Ballard dining-room stared at each other with blanched faces. Then as a cry came from the Hasey place, they sprang up.

"It's murder! He's killed her!"

They ran from the house, down through the orchard and into the fields where John Ballard and his men were working. The sudden appearanec of the terrified and screaming women made them stop in their tracks.

"Oh, John! He's killed her! She's dead!" wailed his wife.

"Who's killed her? Who's dead?" The man ran to meet her.

"That brute at Hasey's!"

"Come on, men, lively now! Hiram, run for Sawyer! Eben, come with me, and the rest of you rout out the neighbors!

The men scattered on the run. With the women, John and Eben returned to the house to wait for the constable and to keep an eye on the Hasey place. All was quiet there.

Soon the constable drove up and neighboring farmers began to run into the yard, some of them armed with the hoes and implements they had been working with.

Sawyer lost no time. He instructed the crowd to "Keep back" and to do as he said.

"You women," he ordered, "come along to point out the chap if need be." This did not serve to calm their agitation.

At the Hasey place the constable and an officer mounted the piazza and clanged the big brass knocker. The door opened and the big, black-bearded man appeared, his expression one of wonder.

"You're under arrest, sir!" Sawyer grasped his arm.

"Arrested, and for what?" The prisoner's surprise was complete.

Sawyer turned to the shrinking women at the foot of the steps. "This is the man, isn't it, ladies?"

They nodded. "That's him."

"Under arrest for murder, sir, and I'm going to investigate. Your name is Troop, isn't it?"

"No."

"What then? The ladies said your name was Miller Troop."

"No." Light of understanding and amusement crept into his face. "I'm Henry Thorpe, manager of the Miller Troupe. We're out here where it is quiet, practising our productions for next summer's vaudeville season. And what you thought was murder was a scene in one of our star acts." And he burst into hearty laughter. Puzzled faces had been appearing in the hall behind him, and now these took up the laugh.

The constable, taken aback, apologized and released his hold. He turned to look for the women who had raised the alarm. But with crimson faces, those mortified persons were fast making their way back through the guffawing crowd.

The Song of the Hermit

By Frederick D. Griggs

Beside the glowing campfire,
  Neath the tall and stately pines;
When shades of night are falling,
  And the new moon softly shines;
The night wind in the tree-tops,
  And the twinkling stars above;
With the fragrance of the spruces,
  That's the life I love.
Away from smoky cities
  And the hurrying crowds of men;
Away from strife and sadness;
  Never to return again;
Far off in God's own country,
  Brave and happy, strong and free;
Alone in the boundless forest,
  That's the life for me.

The Wreck

By Sumner C. Brooks

HAMMY'S boat, a thirty-foot cat, certainly was a beauty, and Hammy himself was a mighty good sailor, a little reckless maybe, but still a mighty good man with a boat. But Dot Wells and I were tired of hearing him say so; and we, especialy Dot, wanted a chance to take down his vanity.

The big storm—it came August 14. 1888, and the old sailors still talk of it—gave us the chance we wanted. It was a grey morning, the clouds were surging across the sky in great black masses, the sea was all black, with white caps as far as one could see, but there was no rain as yet. Truly it was a wicked day, with promise of worse to come, and we should have known better, but Dot and I dared Hammy to take us over to Cottage City and back; and he, although he too knew better, took our dare.

Old Ben Draper heard us speak of our scheme, and knowing us to be the young fools that we were, whipped out, "Ef yer young idiots git outside 'er the jetty terday, yer'll never git in agin; the tide'll cut yer onter the Nobsque reef an' yer'll go all ter smash. Yeu stay in here an watch yer hair grow." And old Eldred, the postmaster, started to say some warning word to us, but Hammy muttered something about "old grumblers," and "not being a squealer," and walked off toward the dock. "Come on you," he shouted, and, excitedly, Dot and I followed.

Under four reefs the stout little Helen worked out of the harbor. The tide was with us, running out through the narrow channel like a mill-race, and Nobsque point to the southeast cut off the worst force of the wind. Slowly we beat to windward; out past Nobsque, with its stunted trees, the little red lighthouse and fog bell, with the huge breakers hissing and foaming among the ugly black boulders at its foot, out past the bell-buoy on the reef, where occasionally an ugly black boulder would show in the trough of a wave. As we passed far to leeward the bell-buoy clanged dolorously with a muffled beat that we heard only occasionally above the roar of white caps and the screams of the wind as it whined through the rigging.

It surely was an ugly day. Again and again a huge, dirty black comber would rush at us, seeming to snarl at us with a white gleam as of cruel teeth; again and again the staunch little boat rode the breakers, and sank down, down into an apparently bottomless trough, only to meet another great, angry wave. The tide had changed and was running with the wind, as we knew it would do before we reached the rips; but yet we were drenched through and through and blinded with spray long before we finally rounded East Chop and made for the breakwater. But our feeling of relief was short lived. A bungling skipper had let his two-master drag anchor, and there she was, right across the mouth of the jetty, breaking up fast, but still just as thoroughly blocking the entrance to the harbor as would a whole mountain.

So we had to turn around and start for home. Scarcely had we started back, running before the ever-increasing gale, when Hammy leaned over and screamed into my ear, "The rain," and pointed to windward. Surely enough, Cape Pogue was hidden in a dense bank of dull grey—the rain. In a minute Edgartown seemed to melt away into the mist; and in another minute we were alone, shut off from the world in a roaring chaos of wind and waves. But Hammy was undismayed. He'd get us in safe all right, he said. I was afraid, although for Dot's sake I pretended to trust in Hammy. Poor Dot's bravado had given out, and she sat crumpled up under the weather rail shivering and miserable, and sobbing bitterly.

For apparently endless hours we sat thus. During our long beat to windward the tide had run out, and now was coming in again, and against the wind. Of course, I can never know surely, but I think we went through the worst place in the whole channel rips. The poor little boat reared like mad; the spray came inboard in solid sheets. Desperately Dot and I set to work bailing to help the boat to clear itself of water. Even Hammy gave in to fear, and when the captain is afraid, hope is small. But even the rips were soon passed, and again we sailed madly on, not knowing where we were, or how far we had come.

Suddenly, close by, sounded the ghastly clangor of the bell-buoy—we were almost on top of the reef, but, thank heaven, to the leeward. Quickly Hammy brought the boat a little nearer the wind, and all three of us hove in the main sheet. With all our strength we could gain but a few inches. Then just astern of us a huge wave broke, and in the following trough we caught one shuddering glimpse of the top of the reef; then it disappeared.

Suddenly Hammy gave a sob of relief. Through a rift in the driving rain he had caught a glimpse of the light on the gas-buoy, he said, and easing off the sheet he headed for the harbor mouth. We all began to hope again.

But in an instant our hopes were dashed. Almost in the same second, the fog-bell on Nobsque dinned on our ears during a lull in the wind, and through a rift in the rain the red secter of Nobsque glared horribly in our blanched faces. We were almost on the rocks of Nobsque! Hammy moved first. With a sudden scream he leaped to his feet and put the helm over hard, but heading for the harbor. There was his fatal move. For the fraction of a second the sail hung idly in the wind, and then, bellying inboard, with the full force of the gale behind it, leaped madly toward us. The heavy boom struck Hammy fairly in the head, and without a sound he disappeared. There was but one possible end to that wild jibe. As the sail brought up sharply to leeward the mast snapped like a straw. The next instant the whole boat seemed to melt and disappear. I caught one wild glimpse of Dot struggling in the wreckage, and then I remember no more.

I came to in the little red house of the lighthouse keeper, who had found me and had slowly coaxed me back to life.

In the bright calm of the morning after the storm they had found Dot among the rocks just below the fog-bell; near her was Hammy's cap, but Hammy they never found.

The M. A. C. Literary Monthly

Editorial Board

-The subscription price of this magazine is $1.00 a year. Single copies, 15 cents.

Contributions are earnestly solicited from all undergraduates. All contributions should be addressed to the Editor of The M. A. C. Literary Magazine, and should be in his hands before the 12th day of the month.

Entered as Second-class Matter, Feb. 1, 1910, at the Post Office, Amherst, Mass.

Editorials

OUR little craft, The Literary Magazine, had barely begun its voyaging under the piloting of its founders when these pilots found it necessary to relinquish the wheel. The magazine, though scarcely more than launched, quickly gathered way under the retiring board, and the new board hopes for a continuance of fair winds and fortunate adventures, that the "Lit" shall carry many cargoes through many years. The first officers retire with the achievement to their credit of having shown the magazine to be seaworthy and of having commanded with dignity and high standards of duty. , So to continue will be the aim of those who now assume direction.

*   *   *   *   *

SIMULTANEOUS with the stirring "Call of the Country Parish," appealing to the sound, strong and high ideals in man, comes the story of a New England pastor who for months has received no salary. As a result he and his family have been forced to live impoverished and humiliated. We question whether this is not an extreme case, but we have no doubt that many such cases exist, differing from this one only in degree. The town of four thousand population having eight or more congregations, each struggling under a heavy debt and unable to pay either a regular or an adequate salary to its minister is as common as it is unedifying.

Meantime, from Canada comes a suggestion for unifying the church. Its details we do not know; but if its object is the consolidation of the many denominations, enabling the united church people of a town to build a church of such architecture as would indicate a developed esthetic sense and to engage one minister of the ability of him whom President Butterfield sees in his vision—giving him more opportunity and more incentive—if the Canadian plan promises to give us this instead of the present restricted denominational work, it is deserving of thoughtful study. To M. A. C. men it should be of especial significance, for to them especially was addressed "The Call of the Country Parish."

*   *   *   *   *

IN a recent discussion of the relation of immigration to the farm, the fact was pointed out that immigrants settling upon farms have less opportunity to become Americanized than their brethren in the cities have. At the very door of M. A. C. are a large number of foreign-born farmers, thrifty and apparently eager to improve, yet in no wise reached or influenced by the college that renders so much service to thousands of other farmers more distant from it. One attempt has been made by M. A. C. students to serve these new New Englanders. It failed, but the problem deserves further study. Obviously it is wise to direct immigrants to the farm rather than to congested cities. Obviously, too, machinery must be provided to teach these strangers our English speech, to acquaint them with our institutions and to explain to them the conditions of success. Such work is peculiarly the mission of M. A. C. men. The attempt to establish country schools and clubs for the purpose of Americanizing our foreign-born farmers should not be abandoned because of a single failure, nor of repeated failures. The opportunity for rendering social service is at our doors.

The

M. A. C. Literary Monthly

| Vol. I | MAY, 1910 | No. 4 |

When Winter Flees

By Nils. P. Larsen

The sun has crimsoned new the east,
The morn is clear, the earth is pleased.
Into the woods—gay, jubilant—
My spirit fresh moves dominant.
The trees stand tall, majestic, grand—
Erst grave kings of a solemn land;
But, breathless through their branches bare,
The faint wind makes mute music there.
I bend my head, in joy I hear
The chirp of birds, glad, free, and near.
Wondering, I cast about my eyes,
And see how faint-heart winter flies.
Beneath my steps the grass is green;
On early limbs, first leaves are seen
Peeping and wondering, is time come
To laugh, and brave old winter glum?
To drippling brooklets then I turn,
Newly awakened in the burn;
Beside the sparkling streamlet there,
I spy the violet, pure and fair,
The Mayflower, and the bluet best.
Ah! now life's life with keener zest.

All in a Summer's Work

By Leon Terry, 1912

"**S**O you are quite decided to go back tonight?" queried Mr. Judson, a rotund little man, with eyes shining cunningly out of a fat face, and always mopping off sweat with a red bandanna handkerchief. He continued: "As I say, Mr. Tucker, I am sorry you can't stay with me. There would be a good future for you here; there is the quarry and the saw-mill and the boxshop, and, of course, always the hogs. Anyway, you are studying agriculture, and I would give you $1500 a year to start with, and maybe an interest in the business. And hogs are going up, too, all the time. Yes, siree! Well, you just think it over, and I'll be going to the postoffice."

And Mr. Judson walked, or rather rolled, out of the room. He was the king of the little hilltown, and was ambitious to have the best farm, the best hogs, the best everything in town. Acting mostly on this principle, he had married the handsomest girl in the county, a school teacher, and graduate of Smith College. And he was almost as proud of her as of his prize-winning stock.

When this very energetic person had vanished, the other two at the table continued their supper in silence. The sun, low in the west, was pouring its rays through the open window and lit up gloriously the golden hair and deep wine-brown eyes of Mrs. Regina Judson.

She was looking straight ahead at Tucker, who had worked for her husband during the summer vacation. But Tucker did not even glance up at Mrs. Judson. They seldom talked, for Tucker both pitied and half despised her. Even now he was thinking:

"Yes, I made a shrewd guess in keeping away from you all through the summer. So your Smith College education is troubling you, after all, and you are not satisfied with that fat . . . person. Though you chose him so as to have comfort the whole of your life, yet now you would like to have someone else make love to you. Well, I would hardly care to take the job . . ."

Supper over, Tucker was smoking a cigar on the veranda steps and watching the sun, just setting beyond the lake. Mrs. Judson came out, and sitting down, asked him:

"I suppose you are glad to be going back to college?"

Perhaps it was the beauty of the quiet evening or the satisfaction he felt that the summer's work was over, but he answered warmly:

"Yes, I *am* glad to be going back. There is much work to be done. This is my last year, and next spring I will graduate and be a free man. And then . . ."

"And then you will have so much fun. The informals, and of course Hamp is so near . . . Boys used to come over pretty often when I was at Smith. And the girls like you, don't they, Mr. Tucker?"

"No, I don't go to Hamp very often. I used to when I was a freshman, and I met a lot of girls there; some were bright, and some were just girls; some took life seriously, and some called me John the second time I met them; and surely I gave them no cause for such familiarity."

Mrs. Judson began to laugh. She had a low, quiet laugh that seemed to flow with a slow ripple into your soul, and nestle there.

"Yes, I am quite sure you gave them no pretext for calling you 'John.' You are not fond of flirting, and yet you are so strong and manly that girls must be falling in love with you all the time. I shouldn't think it would be hard for you to find the right one . . . That is, unless you have already found her?"

"Why, of course I wouldn't let any girl call me by my first name, unless I loved her more than anybody else; more than my future, my honor, the whole world, all this . . ." With his hand he swept the view before them, the broad, placid lake, from which light fog was rising; the western sky now rapidly darkening, and the first star just twinkling timidly and tenderly. "But that will never happen—lightning does not strike in the same place twice. Let me tell you . . ."

Tucker puffed a few times at his cigar, and then said, abruptly:

"When I went away to college I could hardly read and write, though I was of age and was engaged to be married. I had to work and study at the same time, and it wasn't easy . . . Well, the girl waited for me just two years, and then married the village storekeeper. That was four years ago, and now she has three kids. It was a common enough ending; she wrote me a sixteen-page letter, and said on the last page, that he was a better provider. At the time it affected me badly, but now I can smile when I think of the whole sordid affair. I am safe now; after you see the strings the puppets don't amuse you."

He threw away his cigar, as if it tasted bitter, and gazed moodily at the ground. Mrs. Judson also was looking down, though her heart beat furiously. She was glad Tucker was speaking to her so sincerely.

At last she said: "I am happy that we are parting as friends, for I haven't many friends, and all summer you have behaved as a stranger. Won't you tell me, as you would a friend, just what you think of me?"

She half smiled, as she said this, but, glancing at her, Tucker noticed a very wistful, longing look in her eyes, and in spite of his better judgment, he answered to their appeal:

"I had a dog once that went in swimming on a hot day. A big freshet came and carried Jip over the dam. Still he managed to swim near the shore, but some boys started throwing rocks at him. All cut up, and struggling against the fierce current, he finally reached the shore, crawled out . . . and died."

"But I don't see the bearing. I must be stupid. Won't you explain your story?"

But Tucker silently gazed ahead. The forest across the lake moved closer, and looked darkly over the cliffs. The wind blew lightly and coolly. The sky was all sombre but for one rosy bank of clouds. A big night bird flew out of the quiet night and silently hovered on high.

Tucker leaned a little forward. Near the side of his head was a little foot, swinging lightly. The white skin showed through the modest black stocking. Tucker turned away his head.

It grew darker and rather chilly. Then Mrs. Judson said low and quietly: "Won't you get my coat, Johnnie?"

"Poor girl," thought Tucker; "she will never reach shore." He rose, went into the house and brought the coat. Mrs. Judson was standing when Tucker handed her the coat.

"It *is* getting cool, Mrs. Judson," he said, "I have to be starting for my train now."

A tremor seemed to pass through her; she caught at the railing just as Judson stumbled up the veranda steps, exclaiming, "Pork's gone up a half a cent!"

*   *   *   *   *   *   *   *

Tucker was staring into the darkness through the window of the east-bound train. "Wipe the slate clean, and start all over again," he thought. "But she will never reach the shore. And I, too, had to throw a stone—poor girl!"

One Tendency of the Modern Play

By Julius Matz

THE modern play, which means drama, comedy and musical comedy, is of great value, not only for its direct suggestiveness by means of the object lessons it gives in morals and virtue, but also for its indirect bearing upon mind and character. Among modern plays, not a few show a psychological tendency, or rather possess a psychic element. This is found in many of the latest plays, which therefore open the more mysterious corners of the human heart and soul for those who are inclined to think. The influence of such plays may be termed indirect because they usually attempt to reveal some hitherto obscure psychological trait, or to show character as it is formed or misformed by psychological and spiritual influences rather than merely by external facts. They constitute a drama of the mind.

It would be unwise to say that the plot in the plays produced today always has great importance. Many of the best recent plays have almost no plot, so far as incident and outward action go—the action of events. We do not any more expect the author to kill the villain, in the last act or elsewhere; nor to reward the young lover with his—momentary—heart's desire.. What many of us now like in a play is, the exposure of the villain's characteristics, of his strange traits and peculiarities. We want to study his peculiar moral gearing as we see his wheels go round. We may, indeed go further and say that many playgoers have long since lost their interest completely in the villain and the passionate lover. We have done away with the hero of deeds as the chief character on the stage; characters such as we meet on the street, in the parlor and in the office—or rather we ourselves—often occupy the first place on the stage of today. Even in musical comedy the ordinary person frequently appears prominently as a character. Contemporary play-writers and actors are studying and are attempting to make plain those impulses which are behind human strife and actions, especially the strife and action of familiar life.

Those who have seen "The Music Master," in which David Warfield has now played four years, will recall that the acme of the play is reached, not by the development of "story," nor through the culmination of extraneous occurence. The point of highest interest in the play is that which is devoted to a deep psychological demonstration that shows us amazingly what is taking place in the heart of the chief character. The music master is in the home of the man who robbed him of his wife and child. Facing his child, and realizing that he can bring disgrace and evil upon her by making himself known as her father, he leaves,—the secret kept in his heart.

Abraham's leading his only son, Isaac, to the altar for the sake of his God was a demonstration of noble devotion; but a poor, lone, aged father's sacrificing his own happiness for the welfare of his child is a sign of nobler devotion. It is not merely the nobility of the old man that impresses us, it is also the analysis of that undefinable emotion, father-love.

"Clarice," a play written and performed by William Gillette, is a play without "plot," and without important outward incidents; yet it received the greatest ovation. In this play, too, the interest is in the inner, not the outer life. A doctor, in love with Clarice, denies his love because he knows that he will not make her happy. Such contraversions of feelings arouse earnest thought, and so stimulate deeper study of the complexity of human nature and the meaning of human life.

Numerous plays now on the stage present clearly change taking place in character as the action develops. There is less shifting of scenes, less creating of "incident"—because the play is no more a story, a series of events, but a vista of the heart, the spiritual history of one great moral deed.

There are plays, written especially to fit the ability and personality of certain actors, that more than any others, represent this modern type. They are strongly personal, they lay the greatest emphasis upon character, and they are keenly analytical. "The Man from Home," in which William Hodge is the central actor, is a fair example. Robert Edeson, in the "Noble Spaniard," presenting a most queer and striking character, affords further example in making more clear the persistent, whimsical character of the man he represents. Even the comic characters of the vaudeville stage show us this tendency. The comedian is no longer the fool of the ancient plays. Eddy Foy, Louis Mann, Lew Fields, Harry Lauder, are not clowns, but artists. Their work on the stage is, to show us pictures not merely of the outer, but also of the inner man with the greatest detail and exactness.

Jimmie Griggs' Success

By Albert R. Jenks

HURRY up with the breakfast, Sarah."

The words were harshly spoken by Hiram Griggs to his wife, when he came in from doing his morning's chores.

"What is your hurry this morning, Hiram?" asked Sarah, quietly.

She felt more like revolting from the tyrannical rule of her husband than of sympathizing with him.

"Oh! I suppose that I have got to go to town this morning and see if I can get some men to help hay it. The grass is all nearly ready to cut. If Jimmie would get out and do half as much work a day as I do, there'd be no need of my getting extra help this summer. The crop's going to be very poor."

In a gentle voice Sarah began to speak for her ambiitous son, Jimmie; he was already doing a man's work in the field, although he was only 17 years old. His greatest ambition was to go to an agricultural college. Jimmie had worked hard on the farm from boyhood, and had with difficulty finished his high school course. He had tried to introduce up-to-date methods on the home farm, but his tyrannical father rejected all his plans. Jimmie was left to his dreams of success in a little workshop over the wagon shed.

Jimmie's room had a window that opened on the roof, so that he could easily crawl out after he was supposed to have gone to bed, and enter his shop. There Jimmie had spent many an evening working out plans, reading and studying, and he had amassed no small amount of knowledge, which he would like to put to use. His father, however, would do nothing different from what his father and grandfather had done; therefore Jimmie's plans were always shattered.

Jimmie was thinking of going to college in the fall, even though he had to run away to do it; and he was eagerly waiting for a chance to do something which would convince his father that he was right. While his father and mother were discussing the need of extra help, Jimmie came in from doing his morning's chores.

"Why don't you buy or hire an up-to-date mowing machine and hay-rake?" he said, eagerly. "I will run them both, and the two of us can easily handle our crop this year, if only there's a week more of good weather," he added.

"Hm! A lot you know about running those machines. You're just looking for a chance to ride around instead of getting out and doing your share of the work. Why, if I put a mowing machine in my lots, there would be a two-inch stubble left all over my fields. Think I'm going to waste one-fifth of my crop? Father used to say that hand-raked hay was worth $5.00 more a ton than horse-raked hay. Likely I'll let you try your foolish ideas here on my farm. If you would spend half the time in work that you put on dreaming, I might be able to lay up a few dollars a year."

Nothing more was said; Hiram's word was law.

Hiram went to town and spent the day looking for help; but as there was a good demand for help just then, and as he would not pay current wages, he got no help. When his father got home, Jimmie had the chores all done.

Little was said at the supper table, but all were doing a lot of thinking. After supper, Jimmie asked his father how much it would cost him to hire help at the price he had intended to pay.

"Well, I couldn't get off without at least $75.00."

"Will you give me $60.00 for the job if I do it, but do it by machine? You'll have to furnish the old team and your own labor for a week."

Jimmie's father did some thinking much quicker than he was used to doing it. He hated to let the grass spoil and he hated to give in to Jimmie. At last he gave in to his passion. "No, I won't. I'd be out the $60.00 and the grass too, unless I did all the work myself. I won't waste my money just to let you show what a fool you are."

They spent two days in the hayfield; they spoke hardly an unnecessary word. Again Hiram went to town in search of help. He felt confident that he would get it and by so doing turn the tables on his son. But his efforts were vain; the workmen all knew the length of a day's work demanded by him and the amount of pay it would earn.

Sunday morning Jimmie renewed his offer. Hiram went to the window and looked out. His waving fields of blossoming grass were before him. He stood a long time silent. It was a time of struggle—a chance of saving his grass against the certainty of yielding a prejudice. At last he turned.

"It is just in its prime now, Jimmie," he said, sheepishly, "and,—I guess that I will let you go to work in the morning."

No happier moment had Jimmie ever known.

"Where's your machines?" Hiram asked, sharply.

"Mr. Green's grass is never ready when ours is. I went to see him about hiring his machines. He won't need them for a week and he agreed to let me have them for $10.00," replied Jimmie.

"Well, you'll break your neck, or bang up the machines, or spoil the grass or do something else. . But go ahead. You won't believe me till you've tried it. Maybe I can save as much hay as I would have saved the other way. There isn't any other way out of it now."

Jimmie spent the rest of Sunday in looking over the fields and laying plans for the week's work. Monday morning found Jimmie up, chores done, and the mowing machine running before breakfast. As the weather promised to remain good, he laid down all the field. His father cut in the corners, and even caught a happy mood from the unceasing clatter of the knives. By night the field was cocked up, and the next field was laying flat. Hiram acknowledged to his son that it was mowed as clean as he or his father could have mowed it.

Jimmie went to bed early and slept as only farmer's sons can sleep. Tuesday proved a fine hay day; the only thing to mar Jimmie's satisfaction was his running into a hornet's nest towards evening. "Father said he'd get stung," said the boy, half sarcastically. "It appears that I'm the one."

By Wednesday night more than half the hay was in. On Thursday, Jimmie cut the rest of the meadow, much against his father's wishes.

Friday proved lowry, and the meadow grass did not dry out rapidly. Mr. Green, however, offered his help and the use of his tedder. But "thunder heads" began to rise and to flit across the horizon. Jimmie constantly teddered the hay and soon after dinner it was ready to rake. If only the shower would hold off till evening, the hay would all be in. But the clouds drew nearer and nearer; a hard shower was inevitable. Two teams, however, were fast carting the hay into the barn. At five o'clock only two loads remained in the field. The storm was near at hand, however, and thunder could be heard; the sun was hid. Mr. Green called his hired man to help. Everyone hurried as if he had not already done a big day's work. On the racks the hay piled up swiftly. Would they win? They were loading the last load, but the lightning was darting here and there and the thunder was bellowing in all parts of the heavens. Raindrops began to fall. Could thev make it? Only five more "tumbles," and the field would be cleared.

The five "tumbles" were on; men and wagons then rushed for shelter. Scarcely had they reached shelter when the rain began to pour; and it continued to pour all night. The color of all the outstanding neighbor's hay was ruined.

That night Jimmie's joy knew no bounds. He had accomplished what he set out to do; he had " 'shown' Father." But what would come of it after all? Had Father "seen"? When good weather returned, Jimmie and his father helped Mr. Green to get in his hay.

Jimmie followed up his recent success. His father consented to the purchase of a good windmill, a good cultivator, and other labor-saving machinery. Moreover, when Jimmie was paid for his big week's work, he received $100.00 instead of the $60.00; his father said that timely cutting had added quality to the hay.

Nor was that all. About the first of September, Jimmie was called into the sitting-room one evening by his father. To his surprise, his father made several offers in regard to his future. He, seriously considering them all, gave up his hope of a four-year's course at the agricultural college. Instead he staid at home as a partner with his father and took the ten-week's course which was offered at the college in January of the next year.

The farm prospered as a result of hard work and better methods. When questioned about his success, Jimmie always lays it to the mowing machine coupled with good weather.

The Importance of the Study of Rural Sociology

By Samuel W. Mendum

IN the last forty years the agricultural resources of this country have been vastly developed: new fields have been opened up by the railroads; changes in the lines of agriculture in various districts have been brought about by competition; our agricultural colleges have scattered all over the country a band of enthusiastic and intelligent workers; the United States Department of Agriculture and the experiment stations, through their scientific investigations and widely spread reports, have greatly increased the efficiency of the industry. With this increased efficiency have come many of the comforts and advantages enjoyed by people in the cities; the farmer was never so well off as he is today. Yet there are many deficiencies: country life does not measure up to its possibilities.

Notwithstanding all the improvement in the conditions in the country, there is a strong spirit of unrest among the farmers.

Some of the sources of this unrest are obvious. Disregard of the inherent rights of the soil-worker by speculators in lands, monopolistic control of natural resources, and restraint of trade, against which the farmer, alone, unorganized, can poorly defend his interests; poor highways and difficult intercommunication; failure to appreciate soil depletion and its effects; the difficulties involved in the agricultural labor problem; the hard and unrelieved life of the women of the farm; unsanitary conditions and equipment in the country;—these are pointed out in the report of the commission on country life as the main *special* deficiencies in country life.

For these deficiencies the remedies lie with *all* the people, working together through the government, through organizations, and through individual effort, for the common end. "The problem of country life is one of reconstruction; temporary measures and defense work alone will not solve it." The underlying problem is how to develop and maintain on our farms a civilization in full harmony with the best American ideals. This means that the business of agriculture must be made to yield a reasonable return to those who follow it intelligently; and that life on the farm must be made permanently satisfying to intelligent, progressive people."

But in order to deal intelligently with any situation we must know the underlying facts. In dealing with the problem of country life, we must study for ourselves the actual conditions in the country, general and local. Only when we know these actual conditions can we understand the causes for them and perceive the means of improving them. We must have this knowledge of conditions if we wish to act intelligently upon the suggestions of others; we must know how to use our tools.

Nor is the study of the conditions of country life and its institutions a matter for consideration on the part of only those who intend to go to the country; it is a matter for all intelligent people. Farmers, business men, professional men, students, ministers, legislators, will all find pleasure and profit in it. All the people are to help in rural betterment; all the people should study the means of accomplishing this betterment.

Herein lies the importance of the study of rural sociology.

How to Tell a Duck from a Chicken

By R. N. Hallowell

IF you would tell a duck from a chicken, after persuading someone who can tell them apart to place them side by side on a barn-yard roost, within easy sight and hearing; give the feet of each a casual examination. You will note that those of one are webbed and that those of the other are not. You may feel certain that the web-footed bird is a duck and that the other is a chicken. If, however, the feet of neither bird are webbed (some duck owners cut the webs from their ducks' feet in order that they may not swim), give one of the birds a kernel of corn. The other bird will at once quack or make a sound unlike a quack, to let you know that it, too, desires a kernel of corn. If it quacks, you may feel certain that it is a duck; if it makes a sound other than a quack, you may be sure that it is a chicken.

Or to distinguish a duck from a chicken, you may visit each in its own haunts; for ducks and chickens will not come to you to be classified. You will find neither ducks nor chickens on Boston Common or on the dome of the State House or on the Harvard College campus; in fact, you will rarely find a duck or a chicken in any urban community. Therefore, seek the duck and the chicken on the country farm—seek them in the early morning, when the sunlight is bright enough to permit of no mistake in identification; and use the simple key to their classification that I have given you.

Life

MAN comes into this world without his consent and leaves it against his will. During his stay on earth, his time is spent in one continuous round of contraries and misunderstandings. In his infancy, he is an angel; in his boyhood, he is a devil; and in manhood, everything from a lizard up. In his duties, he is a fool. If he raises a family, he is a chump; if he doesn't, the world pities him. If he is a poor man, he is a poor manager and has no sense; if he is rich, he is dishonest, but considered smart. If he is in politics, he is a grafter and a crook; if he is out of politics, you can't place him—he is an undesirable citizen. If he goes to church, he is a hypocrite; if he stays away from church, he is a sinner. If he gives to foreign missions, he does it for show, and if he does not give, he is a tight wad. When he first comes into the world, everybody wants to kiss him. Before he goes out, everybody wants to kick him. If he dies young, there was a bright future before him; if he lives to a ripe old age, he is in the way and is only living to save funeral expenses. Life is a queer proposition. You may consider yourself lucky if you get out of it alive.

The M. A. C. Literary Monthly

The subscription price of this magazine is $1.00 a year. Single copies, 15 cents.

Contributions are earnestly solicited from all undergraduates. All contributions should be addressed to the Editor of The M. A. C. Literary Magazine, and should be in his hands before the 12th day of the month.

Entered as Second-class Matter, Feb. 1, 1910, at the Post Office, Amherst, Mass.

Editorials

BEFORE the next issue goes to press, M. A. C. students will be asked, Can M. A. C. support a literary magazine? The answer will largely be influenced by the esteem in which the experimental attempt of the "Lit" is held. It does not behoove us to help shape the verdict; our opinion is liable to be considered biased. It would benefit no one to deceive ourselves at this juncture, and it is part of wisdom to get unbiased, competent criticism of our past achievements. We therefore cheerfully grant the floor to Professor Neal to review four months of the "Lit."

*   *   *   *   *

CAN M. A. C. support a literary magazine?
Four issues of the "Lit" answer the question. Notwithstanding the numerous difficulties that always lie in the way of new undertakings of the sort, M. A. C. *has* supported a magazine—one of which we may be proud.

I do not mean that the "Lit" has been perfect; in this, that, or the other thing, it might suffer by comparisons. But for a newly founded periodical, it has been all that we could reasonably expect it to be. Indeed, I think it has been more than any prudent prophet would have forecast; it has been more than we who encouraged it would have been satisfied with. And the best thing in its record is, the evidencing of possibilities: what the "Lit" plainly can be is worth time, money and effort upon.

The most immediate danger that the "Lit" must meet is, lack of money. Yet, without soliciting advertising or alumni subscriptions, the students have maintained it half a year. With the recognition of the magazine as a permanent part of our college life, and with the formulation of a permanent business policy, the financial difficulties should be minimized.

A second danger is more remote, yet greater—lack of worthy copy. Yet this danger is perhaps less than some anticipated. The response on the part of individual students to the need of the magazine has been ready. The magazine has had copy for every issue; it has had a good deal of copy that was good, and some copy that was better than good. Every article in the present issue was written expressly for the "Lit," and more copy was offered than could be used.

Evidently in M. A. C., as elsewhere, the scientific spirit broadens minds and deepens sympathies. Evidently M. A. C. stands for things immaterial as well as for things material; the college has a place for a literary magazine, and the men to make it.

Next year, moreover, the literary support ought to increase. Nineteen eleven has men of various interests; 1912 has a considerable number of men who can do work of good literary quality; and 1913 has already put forward a number of men who incline naturally to the literary expression of their ideals. Good material ought to be plenty.

More men should find an interest in the magazine, too, with the introduction of more criticism. The "Lit" has been too exclusively confined to fiction and verse. In the present number a hint is given of the possibilities of the magazine as a periodical of discussion. It can readily become our local exchange for ideas. Many a man knows intimately some one thing about which many other men would like to know. Criticism, the presentation of individual thought, the interchange of ideas, will add much to the usefulness of the "Lit."

What next, then? The first period of the magazine's existence is over. Shall it have a second? The four experimental numbers seem to give sufficient answer. Let the "Lit" go on.

CPSIA information can be obtained
at www.ICGtesting.com
Printed in the USA
BVHW041426090119
537419BV00011B/199/P

9 780483 538054